I Live
to
Love

S a r a h   R a e   G i l b e r t

Published by Redwood Publishing, LLC
www.RedwoodDigitalPublishing.com

For more information, contact:
Sarah Rae Gilbert
www.daisytherottie.com
contact@daisytherottie.com

ISBN Hardcover: 978-1-947341-07-4
ISBN Paperback: 978-1-947341-06-7
ISBN eBook: 978-1-947341-05-0

Library of Congress Control Number: 2017956504

Cover Design and Illustrations by Nancy Batra
Interior Design by Ghislain Viau

I dedicate this book to all the readers I've met and have yet to meet.
Let it fill your heart with love, hope, and compassion.

Hello, my friend. How do you do?
My name is Daisy and I'm just like you.

I may not eat veggies or wear fancy clothes.

I don't have two thumbs. I don't walk on my toes.

But I do have a heart and you have one too,
And with that we can love, and love I do!

I live to love and I love to live.
I have a lot of love to give.

I love to run and leap and bound.
I love to make some funny sounds.

I love my treats and I love my toys.
I love to share with girls and boys.

I love to swim in water so blue.
I love my friends, both old and new.

I love to kiss and I love to hug.

I love to have my belly rubbed.

I love to do what I think is right.
I am here to love, not to fight.

I love it all, so very much,
So many things, a ton, a bunch!

But most of all, I love my mother.
I love my father, sister, and brother.

I love to make them smile so wide.
It makes me feel so good inside!

And yes, it's true, I love you too.
That's a guarantee; I promise you.

I love your heart; I love your mind.
I think you're smart and brave and kind!

So promise me you'll try to bring,
A little love to everything.

When times are tough; when life's unfair,
Spread some love to show you care.

Love can heal and love can grow.

Trust me, friend, this I know!

I live to love. It's what I do!
My name is Daisy and I'm just like you.

Contact Daisy:

www.DaisyTheRottie.com

 www.instagram.com/imdaisytherottie

 www.facebook.com/ImDaisytheRottie